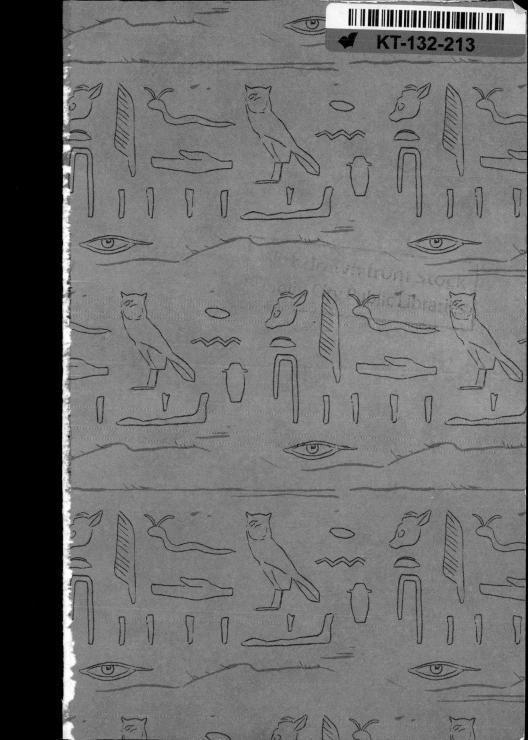

KT-132-213

Withdrawn from Stock
Dublin City Public Libraries

AN INCREDIBLE TRUE STORY

Leabharlann na Cabraí
Cabra Library
01-2228317

2 3 MAR 2023

TUTANKHAMUN'S
TREASURE

DISCOVERING THE SECRET TOMB OF EGYPT'S ANCIENT KING

DAVID LONG

Illustrated by
STEFANO TAMBELLINI

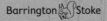

Barrington Stoke

For Finn Barnes

First published in 2022 in Great Britain by
Barrington Stoke Ltd
18 Walker Street, Edinburgh, EH3 7LP

www.barringtonstoke.co.uk

Text © 2022 David Long
Illustrations © 2022 Stefano Tambellini

The moral right of David Long and Stefano Tambellini to
be identified as the author and illustrator of this work has
been asserted in accordance with the Copyright, Designs and
Patents Act, 1988

All rights reserved. No part of this publication may be
reproduced in whole or in any part in any form without the
written permission of the publisher

A CIP catalogue record for this book is available
from the British Library upon request

ISBN: 978-1-80090-007-3

Printed by Hussar Books, Poland

Contents

1

TREASURE

Since the beginning of time, people all over the world have been looking for hidden treasure. Perhaps it's treasure that has been lost by accident or in a natural disaster like an earthquake. Or perhaps it was hidden away to keep it safe from thieves.

There are different ideas about what treasure is. A locked wooden box stuffed full of gold coins and stolen jewels, and dug deep into a hole on a desert island, is the best sort of pirate treasure. But things that are very, very old make good treasure too – things like tools or weapons, or even bits of broken glass and pottery.

Treasure hunters call these objects artefacts. They may not seem as precious as gold or jewels, but they can tell us a lot about the people they once belonged to.

The professional treasure hunters who look for these artefacts are called archaeologists. They are scientists, and their job is to hunt for objects from the distant past. They study the objects they find to learn more about the way ancient people lived on our planet.

Archaeologists are like detectives, and their work can be exciting, but it can also be very dangerous. Sometimes they explore ruins in a rainforest full of poisonous creatures, or they work deep underwater, or miles from anywhere in the middle of a dry, hot desert.

Archaeologists like to find things that people used for their work or in their homes. Sometimes they find human remains (like skulls and skeletons). Sometimes they spend days and months looking at the objects they have found to learn how those ancient peoples grew food or hunted animals, how they lived and what their worlds and beliefs were like.

Bit by bit, archaeologists are able to describe what life used to be like for those ancient peoples. They can compare different civilisations around the world and their tribes and families during different periods of history.

This work is very challenging, and modern archaeologists have to learn many different skills. Often they don't even have an accurate idea about where to start looking for the artefacts that will tell them more about those ancient worlds.

Maps and old documents can sometimes give archaeologists clues about where to start their hunt for artefacts. Metal detectors can help locate tiny objects far beneath the ground. Photographs taken by a high-flying drone can show where an old house or castle once stood, even if the building was burned down or destroyed hundreds of years ago. But archaeologists need a lot of luck too. Some of the most famous and most fabulous treasures were discovered by accident. Archaeologists have found the ruins of palaces in the weirdest places; they have found astonishing wonders just when they had given up and were about to go home.

Sometimes archaeologists waste a lot of time and effort digging in the wrong places or refusing to admit that they have made a big mistake.

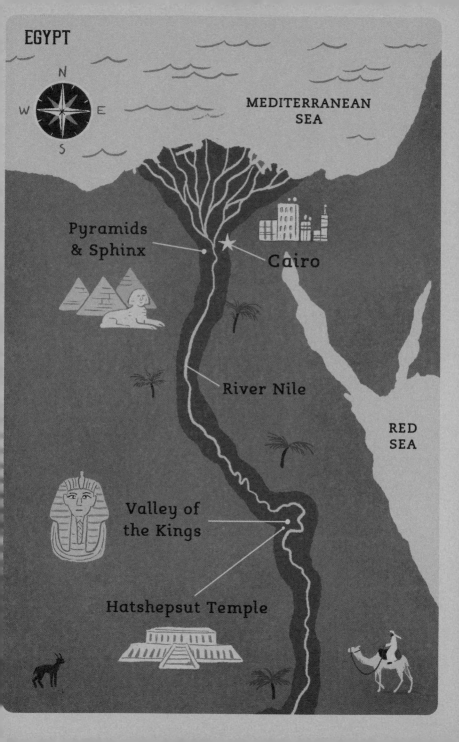

2

ANCIENT EGYPT

Look at Egypt on a map. It stretches from North Africa into the Middle East. It is huge! Most of Egypt is desert even though the longest river in the world flows through it. This river is the Nile, and it is so long that the journey from one end to the other is around

6,670 kilometres. That's the same distance as from the middle of London all the way to India.

For thousands of years, Egypt was one of the richest, most advanced and most exciting civilisations the world had ever seen. Its kings were powerful rulers called pharaohs. They controlled the lives of more than a million ordinary men, women and children, some of whom were slaves.

Most of the pharaohs were men, but there were some women. Some were regents – they ruled Egypt while the real pharaoh was still a child.

The first Egyptians were farmers who settled along the banks of the Nile more than 7,000 years ago. The climate along the River Nile is hot and the land is dry, but the river

floods every year, which makes the soil perfect for growing crops and raising animals such as sheep, goats, pigs and geese.

Over time, simple farming villages grew to become towns, and towns became large and magnificent cities. The powerful Egyptian army fought and invaded the countries nearby and the area of land the pharaohs controlled grew bigger and even richer.

Far out in the burning heat of the desert, people worked hard digging for gold and precious stones to make into beautiful jewellery. Others dug deep channels to control the flow of the mighty Nile. These channels brought fresh water to the fields so that Egypt's farmers could grow even more food. Boats took the food along the Nile to trade with other countries and came home with valuable and beautiful treasures. The gold and precious stones from the mines made the pharaohs some of the richest people who ever lived.

The Egyptians were inventors, artists and craftsmen as well as good farmers and soldiers. They invented a new form of writing called hieroglyphics, which uses small pictures instead of words.

They were talented builders, constructing impressive monuments and lavish temples where priests worshipped more than 2,000 different gods.

They also built enormous tombs called pyramids for their pharaohs. Over a hundred of these pyramids were constructed, and even the smallest took many years to finish. The biggest one, the Great Pyramid of Giza, was the tallest building on Earth and held this record for an incredible 3,800 years.

One of their most famous monuments, the Great Sphinx, was carved out of solid stone,

with the body of a lion and a human head. It is still one of the largest statues ever made at 20 metres high and more than 70 metres long.

The Egyptians wanted their temples and other buildings to be beautiful to look at as well. The walls were often richly decorated with amazing carvings and very detailed, colourful paintings. In fact, many Egyptian buildings were so well made that they are still standing today. Their decorations can tell us a lot about life in Ancient Egypt, even thousands of years later.

The Egyptians left some other extraordinary things behind too, including their famous mummies. A mummy is the name for the bodies that were buried in the pyramids. These belonged to dead pharaohs and to other rich and powerful men and women. They were wrapped in bandages and spices, and because of the dry weather in Egypt, the bodies didn't rot away.

The Egyptians preserved the bodies because they believed in life after death and thought the dead people would carry on using their

bodies. The tombs in the pyramids had many separate rooms. Each room was filled with the things the dead person's family thought the mummy would need in the afterlife: food and wine, clothes (including underwear), furniture, musical instruments, jewellery, wigs and make-up, as well as little statues of the dead person's favourite gods. Some historians believe that slaves were sometimes buried alive when their master or mistress died.

The pyramids and other monuments make Egypt one of the most interesting countries for an archaeologist to explore. Some of the world's most important archaeological discoveries have been made in Egypt, and many museums all over the world have fabulous objects on display that were dug out of the sand and rock close to the Nile. Often these artefacts have come from an important area known as the Valley of the Kings.

3

MOVING TO THE VALLEY OF THE KINGS

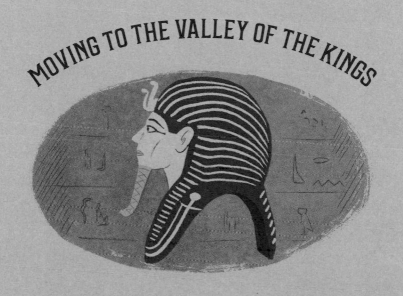

The pyramids are easily the biggest and most famous ancient monuments in Egypt. The tallest and most impressive one, the Great Pyramid of Giza, was built for a pharaoh called Khufu who died nearly 4,600 years ago. It is almost 150 metres tall and one of the Seven Wonders of the World.

Khufu's pyramid was built with 2.3 million blocks of solid stone. These weighed between 1 tonne and 80 tonnes each and had to be cut by hand and moved into position without any machinery. This was a huge and difficult task, and archaeologists think between 20,000 and 30,000 workers were needed to put the blocks in place. Khufu's pyramid weighed nearly 6 million tonnes.

It took more than 20 years to build just this one pyramid even with all those people working on the site. Even the smaller pyramids took a very long time to build. The pyramids were tombs, and the Egyptians often started to build them for the pharaohs when they were young so that they would be finished in time for when the pharaohs died and needed burying.

The pharaoh was the most important person in Egypt, so their tombs had to be amazing. Pyramids were built to protect the pharaoh's dead body from tomb robbers. These robbers spent their lives trying to break into pyramids to steal the gold and other treasures inside. They didn't care about the dead bodies – they just wanted the loot.

If you were caught robbing a tomb, you would be horribly punished and even killed, but the tomb robbers went on trying to break into pyramids to steal the treasure inside because they knew how valuable it was.

One of Khufu's treasures was an entire ship, which was buried next to his pyramid. His body was put deep inside the pyramid itself, in a heavy stone coffin called a sarcophagus. Other pharaohs were buried underneath their pyramids, but to keep their mummies safe, the burial place was top secret. The entrance to each pyramid was hidden too (sometimes it was far underground), and there were sometimes fake rooms or chambers to trick the robbers.

The real chamber with the pharaoh's sarcophagus was almost impossible to get to. You had to crawl along steep, narrow passages or tunnels cut through the pyramid. Once the sarcophagus had been put into the pyramid, the passages were filled with rocks to make it even harder for the robbers to crawl through. But somehow the robbers nearly always succeeded, and we now know that most of the pyramids were broken into not long after they were shut.

Because of this, the Egyptians knew that they had to find another, safer way to bury their rulers. Even the smallest pyramids were massively expensive to build, and if they couldn't protect the mummies and their treasures, there was no point spending so many years building them.

So, more than 3,000 years ago, the Egyptians decided to stop building pyramids and they began to build a very different sort of royal tomb. The first of these new tombs was nearly 500 kilometres south of Khufu's Great Pyramid in a lonely part of the desert. The Egyptian name for the area was Ta-sekhet-ma'at, but today we call it the Valley of the Kings.

This new royal tomb was built for a pharaoh called Thutmose I, and he was the first pharaoh to be buried in the Valley of the Kings. Over the next 500 years, more kings were buried in the same place. Archaeologists have found more than 60 different tombs here, with some examples shown below.

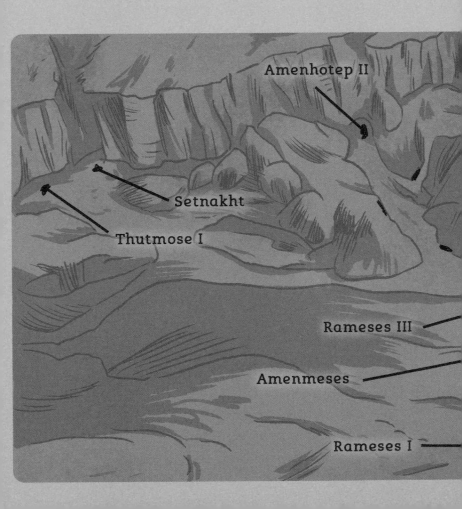

Some of these tombs are just simple holes in the ground with space for only one mummy, but some are very grand and have a hundred or more different chambers inside them. Not all the tombs were used for pharaohs. Some belonged to their queens or to important priests and other rich Egyptians.

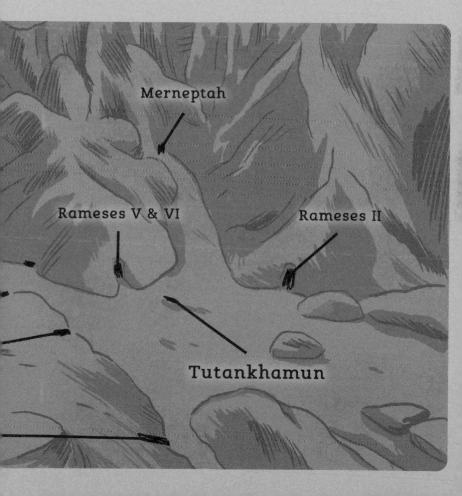

The workers in the Valley of the Kings didn't build grand, towering pyramids. Instead they dug long, winding tunnels or corridors deep into the rock.

Some of the tunnels were more than a hundred metres long. Each one had to be slowly excavated – dug out by hand – together with all the different rooms leading off to the left and right. The most important room was where the dead person's mummy lay in its stone sarcophagus. Other rooms were used to store all the things which the Egyptians believed were needed in the afterlife.

The biggest tombs in the Valley of the Kings were much less showy on the outside than the huge pyramids, but inside they were just as amazing. The finest tombs were very beautiful with hundreds of colourful paintings. The paintings covered the walls of the tunnels as well as the rooms leading off them, and Egypt's

most talented craftsmen carved complex
designs into the stonework.

Everything possible was done to keep the mummies and their treasures safe. No one was allowed into the Valley of the Kings except the people who worked there and the priests who looked after the tombs.

Most of the workers lived in a small village nearby called Set Ma'at. They had to walk to the tombs each morning through the scorching desert. There were only 20 or 30 people working on the tombs to keep things secret. It was not like when the pyramids were being built and there were 20,000 or 30,000 people working together.

Most of the tombs were broken into anyway. No one knows how the thieves found out about the new tombs or how they got into them. For a long time, archaeologists thought the robbers were just ordinary thieves who crept into the Valley after dark. But now people think that perhaps some of the later pharaohs ordered the tombs of their ancestors to be broken into so they could steal the treasures themselves!

Whatever the truth is, experts now know that most of the tombs had already been broken into more than 2,500 years ago. This meant that the pharaohs' treasures were stolen long before a single archaeologist had even heard of the Valley of the Kings. Even so, the Valley of the Kings is one of the most important archaeological sites in the whole world.

The pharaohs' rule came to an end when Alexander the Great conquered their lands in 332 BC. After that, the Romans invaded Egypt and ruled it for hundreds of years. Life in Egypt changed for ever. There were no more new tombs in the Valley of the Kings. The area was abandoned, and for hundreds of years the ancient tombs lay silent and forgotten.

4

HOWARD CARTER

People from Europe started to visit Egypt after France invaded and occupied the country in 1798. European nations had always traded with Egypt and knew about its rich treasures. The visitors came to see the pyramids and the Valley of the Kings. An English explorer called

Richard Pococke drew one of the first proper maps of the area, and the ruler of France, Napoleon Bonaparte, sent more than a hundred scholars, scientists and engineers to search for tombs.

Queen Victoria's eldest son, Bertie – later King Edward VII – visited Egypt in 1862. The prince began to collect curious and exciting objects from the time of the pharaohs.

All around the world, people wanted to know more about Ancient Egypt. They called themselves Egyptologists, and more and more of them began to explore the Valley of the Kings. One of these was a young man called Howard Carter.

Carter was born in London, and his father was an artist. He spent a lot of his childhood with some of his family who lived in Norfolk. A few miles away, there was a grand country house owned by Lord Amherst with one of the world's best libraries of old and valuable books. Next door to this amazing library was a room full of ancient artefacts from Egypt.

Howard Carter was allowed to visit the house whenever he was in Norfolk, and it quickly became his favourite place. He spent as much time there as he could, looking for hours at all the Egyptian treasures and reading everything he could find about Ancient Egypt and the pharaohs.

Lady Amherst saw how interested Carter was and wanted to help him. She had a friend who was an Egyptologist and was working at a burial site in Egypt – somewhere called Beni Hasan. Carter got the job of helping him to keep a careful record of anything that was found in the excavation.

Howard Carter was only 17 when he arrived in Egypt, but he was keen and hardworking and a very quick learner. Carter's father was an artist and had taught him how to paint and draw. Carter used these skills to copy the decorations on the walls of the tombs. Living and working in the desert was hard (it was so hot that the archaeologists often had to eat and sleep inside the tombs), but Carter loved what he was doing.

Making accurate copies of wall paintings was an important part of what the archaeologists were doing. Carter's brilliant drawings began to attract the attention of other important Egyptologists. Soon the young artist was invited to help them with their work too.

One of the places that Carter went to work at was a temple built more than 3,000 years ago for a powerful Egyptian queen called Hatshepsut. Carter was older now, and by working at many different sites he had become an expert archaeologist as well as a fine artist. He was made Chief Inspector of Monuments for Upper Egypt.

Chief Inspector was a very important job. Carter was allowed to run his own expeditions instead of just working as an assistant to other archaeologists. He also had to help other archaeologists run their digs and prevent

tourists picking up objects and stealing them from important sites.

Carter spent six years as Chief Inspector. He worked hard to improve the way archaeologists in Egypt worked, and he set up new and better ways to excavate royal tombs and other key sites. Carter's improvements were important, but they meant archaeology became even slower and even more expensive.

Carter was not a rich man. He made a bit of extra money as an artist, but when he gave up the job as Chief Inspector he didn't know how to pay for any more of the work he wanted to do in the Valley of the Kings.

5

STOPS AND STARTS

Lord Carnarvon was one of a group of rich English lords who spent the winter in Egypt. Most of them went for the warm climate and to visit the exotic ruins and explore the banks of the Nile. Lord Carnarvon was very interested

in archaeology, and in 1906 he and Howard
Carter met for the first time.

Lord Carnarvon was extremely rich and so
was his wife. Their home in England, Highclere
Castle, was even grander than Lord Amherst's
large house in Norfolk. Carnarvon loved motor
racing, but he had a serious accident and went
to Egypt to recover. There he began to find

out about Ancient Egypt and all its treasures, and he became hooked. He was keen to start hunting for more, but he knew that he needed proper help. He decided to employ Howard Carter.

With all that Carter knew about Ancient Egypt already, and with the money that Lord Carnarvon had to spend on the project, the two men made an excellent team, but they had a frustrating wait before they were given permission from the Egyptian government to start digging in the Valley of the Kings.

By the time they did get a permit and could start the dig, many archaeologists thought that there was nothing left for them to discover. They thought Carnarvon was wasting his money, but Carter was sure that there was still treasure to be found. He had become obsessed with the idea that there was still one tomb that no one had discovered yet – and that it was waiting for him to find it.

Carter believed that the tomb was where a pharaoh called Tutankhamun was buried. Carter had learned about him when he had worked for an American archaeologist a few years earlier.

Tutankhamun ruled Egypt more than 3,000 years ago. Today he is the most famous pharaoh of them all, but in Carter and

Carnarvon's day no one knew anything about him. Many Egyptologists thought he wasn't important because he was only on the throne for a few years and was still a teenager when he died.

The greatest pharaohs were all old men like Rameses II, who ruled Egypt for about 67 years, and Thutmose III, who had been king for more than 50 years. These two had been highly successful warriors who built huge temples as well as many other important monuments. Tutankhamun was young and hadn't built much. He had left very little behind.

No one was even sure who Tutankhamun's parents had been or exactly when he died. No one thought he was interesting, but Howard Carter didn't care. He was sure that Tutankhamun's tomb lay hidden somewhere in the Valley of the Kings. He also thought that it was a royal tomb that no robbers had broken into, even thousands of years before.

Carter had almost no proof that Tutankhamun's tomb existed, but Lord Carnarvon found his ideas and enthusiasm very exciting. Carnarvon knew that every single pharaoh's tomb that had been discovered had already been looted – but what if Carter was right about this one? What if they could find a royal tomb that still had its treasures? That would be the greatest discovery that anyone could dream of.

But almost as soon as they started work they had to stop again. The First World War began, and the project had to wait three years. Carter couldn't get back on site until 1917.

6

NO LUCK, NO HOPE

Carter wanted to dig through the great heaps of rock and rubble which were all over the Valley. These had been left by previous archaeological teams. Carter wanted to make sure that the ground under all the rocks and

stones had been properly looked over before the rubble was dumped on top.

Moving all the rubble would have been easy with mechanical diggers and modern bulldozers. But in 1917 the only tools Carnarvon and Carter's Egyptian workmen had were spades and adzes, a special type of axe used for digging. It took a very long time for 50 workmen to dig anything up. Carter warned Lord Carnarvon that it might be months or even years before they found anything. If there was anything left to find ...

Carnarvon understood, and he asked Carter to make a start as soon as possible. Both men felt good about their chances, but they had no idea at that point just how long the digging would take or how much rubble they would need to move before they found anything.

Carnarvon paid Carter and his team of workmen to dig in the Valley for more than five years. By 1922, they had shifted around 180,000 tonnes of rock, sand and rubble, which is about the same as a thousand houses (or 1,500 blue whales).

All of this had to be carried away in baskets. It was hard work and it sounded impressive, but almost nothing had been found in the piles of stones or under them. The main things that Carter had to show were a few small stone pots which had been made when another pharaoh called Rameses II was king. These were interesting and good enough to display in a museum, but they had nothing to do with Tutankhamun.

People think Lord Carnarvon had paid out about a million pounds of his own money by this point. He decided he'd had enough. He sent a letter to Carter asking him to return to England. Carnarvon was going to tell Carter the bad news when he arrived: the hunt for Tutankhamun had to stop.

7

GOOD NEWS AT LAST

Lord Carnarvon was fed up. He still loved Egypt, but by 1922 he had given up hope of ever finding Tutankhamun's tomb. He told his friend Howard Carter he didn't want to spend any more money looking for it.

Carter was devastated by this news. He was determined to carry on. He begged Lord Carnarvon to give him one last go at finding the tomb. He pulled out a map of the rocky landscape showing a very small area where they hadn't dug yet and even said he'd pay back whatever Carnarvon spent on one final dig if they didn't find anything.

Carnarvon knew Carter couldn't afford to do this, but in the end it didn't matter. The

archaeologist's passion and enthusiasm had changed his mind, and Lord Carnarvon agreed that Carter could spend one more winter digging in the Valley of the Kings. Carnarvon would pay all the bills.

Carter was very pleased and went back to Egypt as soon as he could. On 1 November 1922, he and his men entered the Valley and began work for the last time. Carter got them to dig in the area he had shown Carnarvon on the map. This was close to the tomb of another pharaoh called Rameses VI. To begin with, there was nothing to report, but then on 4 November a young Egyptian boy working at the site had an incredible stroke of luck.

The boy was carrying water for the men who were digging to drink. He was looking for a place to put the water down when he tripped and nearly fell. He had tripped over a strange-looking piece of rock, and he stopped to look at it.

The rock was flat and lay at an angle, as if
it had been carved into shape. When the boy
showed it to some of the workmen, they were
excited and began clearing the sand away so
they could have a proper look.

By the time they called Carter over,
everyone was desperate to see more. When
they dug away the sand around the rock the
boy had tripped over, everyone saw that it was
a stone step. The step had been cut into the
rock floor of the Valley, and it looked like it was

very, very old. Carter and the workmen knew that the entrances to the royal tombs in the Valley of the Kings often began with a series of stone steps – maybe this was the tomb they had been looking for all these years.

The men went on digging, and by the next day everyone could see that there were twelve steps leading downwards into the rock. They

were still not at the bottom, but at sunset
Carter went down them and thought he could
see the top of what looked like a doorway. This
was even more exciting – the doorway had been
carefully blocked up with bricks and plaster.

Best of all, Carter could see the pattern of
an oval seal or a stamp in the ancient plaster.
In the seal was a carving of nine slaves with a
type of wild dog called a jackal. Carter knew

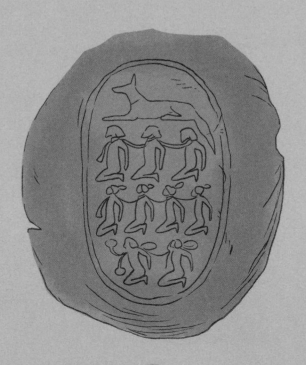

that seals like these were used on royal tombs. The jackal was known as Anubis, the god of mummification, who was said to accompany dead kings into the afterlife. This seal was still unbroken. Could that mean that the tomb had not been robbed?

They must have all wanted to smash down the doorway to see what was on the other side, but archaeologists have to be very careful. Their work has to be done slowly to avoid breaking anything they discover. Carter was very excited, but he wanted to tell Lord Carnarvon what had been found before he went into the tomb.

He told the men to cover the steps back up with sand. He still wasn't sure if this was Tutankhamun's tomb, but he had to make sure that no one else found it and broke into it.

Carter quickly sent a thrilling telegram to Lord Carnarvon. In 1922, this was the quickest way to send messages over a long distance, but as telegrams cost a lot of money, Carter kept his as short as possible:

At last have made wonderful discovery in the Valley a magnificent tomb with seals intact re-covered same for your arrival; congratulations.

Carter had spent more than 30 years looking for Ancient Egyptian treasures in the desert and waiting for this moment. Now he had to wait a little bit longer for his partner to arrive so the two of them could at last see what was behind the mysterious doorway.

8

"CAN YOU SEE ANYTHING?"

When Lord Carnarvon got Carter's telegram, he was just as excited as Carter. He wanted to get to the Valley of the Kings as quickly as possible, but he was at home in Highclere Castle.

In 1922, travelling from one country to another took much longer than it does today. There were no airlines carrying passengers from England to Egypt. Lord Carnarvon had to get a ship across the English Channel, then take a train through France, then get another ship to Egypt, and then another train – and finally a donkey ride for the last few kilometres to the tomb. The journey took around two weeks.

Because of this it was 23 November before Carnarvon finally reached the Valley of the Kings. His daughter, Evelyn, had come with him, and the first thing they did was to congratulate Carter.

The next day was spent clearing the steps again, which took many hours. Now, for the first time, Carnarvon and Evelyn could see there were sixteen steps leading down to the secret doorway with its unbroken seal.

The seal had to be photographed before anyone could go through the doorway. This was so that other Egyptologists could see what it had looked like when it was still in one piece. Without a photo, no one would believe that they had found a tomb with an unbroken seal across its entrance.

After that, Carter and his team went on clearing away rocks and sand until they could see all of the doorway. Now they could see several more seals. These were lower down the door than the first one, and Carter began to think they could be the seals of Tutankhamun. If his hunch was right, Carnarvon's money had not been wasted after all. After years of searching, he might actually have found the tomb of Egypt's boy-pharaoh!

It wasn't all good news, however. The mystery seals were unbroken, but Carter and Carnarvon could see that the doorway had been badly damaged at some point and then repaired. This could mean that Tutankhamun's tomb had been broken into after all. They hoped that it had been quickly closed up again and resealed before everything inside could be stolen.

The next job was to take away the bricks and plaster which filled the doorway. This took a long time too, but at last the doorway was opened up, and Carter and Carnarvon saw

there was a passageway behind it. This led
even deeper underground, but it was full of
stones and other rubble.

Everyone wanted to get into the tomb – the
suspense was unbearable – but the passage
was 9 metres long and they had to spend even
more time clearing it. At last, at the far end,
Carter found yet another secret doorway. This
one was also sealed shut, but with growing
excitement he quickly knocked a small hole
into it near the top. He poked a long metal rod
through the hole, and he could tell there was
a room on the other side of it. A jet of warm
air came rushing out of the room. Perhaps
that was the first air to escape from the inner
chamber for more than 3,000 years.

Carter asked for a candle, which he lit and
held up to the door. The flame flickered in the
warm air, but once it settled down he put it
through the jagged hole to light up the room on
the other side.

"Can you see anything?" Carnarvon asked
him nervously.

Carter's eyes took a few moments to get
used to the dark, but then he replied. "Yes,"
he told his friend, "wonderful things!"

9

THE WONDERFUL THINGS

Carter thought that the tomb had been broken into at least once before, shortly after Tutankhamun's mummy was buried. But the doorway had been sealed up again before everything inside the tomb could be smashed or stolen.

That was why the mummy and its treasures were still in the tomb when Carter and his team broke through. No one had ever before found a royal tomb with so much treasure still in it, and the excitement was incredible.

News of their extraordinary discovery quickly travelled across the world. People everywhere were desperate to hear more about what had been found.

The most amazing item turned out to be a death mask of Tutankhamun's face. It was made out of solid gold and decorated with dark blue lapis lazuli and other precious stones.

The outer coffin: 2.24m long, made of wood overlaid with gold foil; represents the king as the deity Osiris.

The middle coffin: 2.04m long, made of wood and overlaid with gold foil and multicoloured glass.

Today it is one of the most famous museum artefacts anywhere in the world, but that was only one of all the thousands of objects which Carter and Carnarvon and their team found in the tomb.

The inner coffin: 1.88m long, made of solid gold weighing 100.4kg.

The bandaged mummy wearing the famous golden death mask.

Tutankhamun's tomb is one of the smaller ones in the Valley of the Kings. It has only four secret chambers, but even so it was stuffed full of amazing things. As Carter and Carnarvon made their way from one room to the next, they discovered that each one was full of incredible objects.

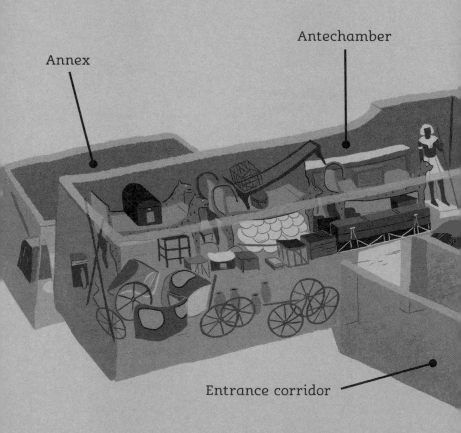

Annex

Antechamber

Entrance corridor

These were all the things Tutankhamun's family and servants thought the mummy would need in the afterlife. There were so many of them that the beautifully decorated rooms weren't large enough for everything to be neatly stacked. Instead it looked as though the objects had been crammed into the tomb as

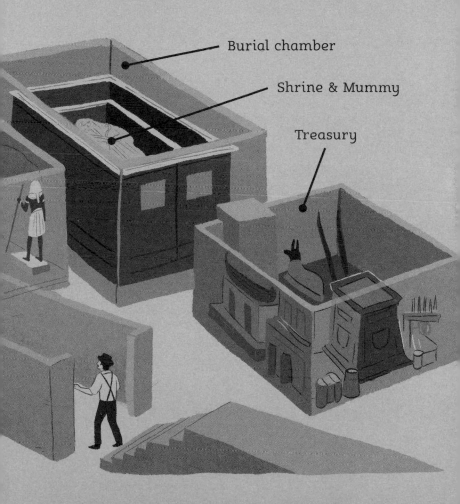

Burial chamber

Shrine & Mummy

Treasury

quickly as possible before the doorways were sealed shut.

Carter couldn't have hoped for a better result. So many different objects would help archaeologists and historians understand much more about life in Ancient Egypt. But emptying the tomb was a massive job for Carter and his workmen.

It took years, not weeks or months, to remove so many old and fragile objects from the tomb. After that, Carter spent many more years studying the objects closely to make an accurate list of what was in the tomb. Altogether it took nearly ten years, until there were more than 5,000 items on Carter's list. Some of them were quite simple things, like pots and bowls with oil, wine and even food in them. Others were far more spectacular, like the gold death mask and a large sarcophagus, or coffin, carved out of red quartzite stone. Carter also found several statues of gods and animals as well as masses of priceless jewellery, a golden bed and other elegant furniture. There was even a chariot! Perhaps the young pharaoh had enjoyed racing, just like Lord Carnarvon.

Carter planned to take as much of the treasure as he could out of Egypt and back to England. He may have wanted it to go on display at the British Museum in London, but the Egyptians refused to allow this.

Carter's amazing discovery had made Tutankhamun the ancient world's most famous ruler, and the Egyptians wanted to keep everything in their own country. Carter had to agree, and today the mummy and its treasures are on display in the capital, at Cairo's amazing new Grand Egyptian Museum.

Even though he gave all the treasures to the Egyptian museums, some experts think that Carter may have stolen a few small things

Artefacts from King Tutankhamun's Tomb

Jewellery
A scarab beetle
brooch & rings

Model boat

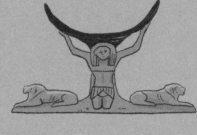

Pillow or head rest

Chair

A golden bed

Sandals

Canopic jars

Trumpet

Gloves

Chariot

from the tomb. We can't be sure about this, but Carter was spotted once trying to hide a small painted sculpture of the boy-pharaoh. Perhaps Carnarvon and Carter wanted some things to keep to help them remember their great adventure together.

Carter gave the sculpture back, but it was all a bit suspicious. Some other small items vanished too – bits of silver, a blue glass vase and a small dog made of ivory. Some of these turned up in museums in Germany and America. Maybe Carter stole things so that he could sell them later.

Even if Carter did want to keep some of the treasures that he had found, it would be surprising to learn that he stole things because he hated it when artefacts were taken from important archaeological sites.

10

IS THERE A MUMMY'S CURSE?

No one will ever know if Howard Carter was a thief, but the other Tutankhamun mystery is the Mummy's Curse.

Some people believe that the ancient Egyptians put a curse or a spell on

Tutankhamun's tomb to protect their dead pharaoh. No one has ever found any evidence for this, although the ancient Egyptians did believe in magic and often said prayers and spells when a mummy was being prepared for burial.

However, some bad things did happen after the famous tomb was opened. People say that Lord Carnarvon's teeth began falling out soon afterwards, but even if this isn't true, he died a few months later, probably from an infected mosquito bite.

Back at Highclere Castle, Lord Carnarvon's favourite dog was reported to have dropped dead at exactly the same time that he did, and then a few years later a member of the digging team was poisoned. Carter's secretary in London died too, then a friend's house burned down, and an Egyptian prince was murdered by his English wife, possibly after visiting the tomb.

This all sounds spooky, but Egyptologists have never taken the Mummy's Curse seriously. Howard Carter thought it was nonsense, but journalists have always found the idea exciting and over the years the stories they reported about the Curse helped to make Tutankhamun even more famous.

Carter felt that everyone who went into the tomb with him came out and was fine. He also said their lives were better than before because they'd been lucky enough to have been part of one of the most incredible archaeological discoveries ever made.

For him and for the other archaeologists working today, the thousands of items found in the tomb are much more interesting than any curse. We still have a lot to learn about Tutankhamun himself – no one is even sure who his mother was – but the contents of his tomb tell us a lot about his life and about the lives of other Egyptians at the time he was pharaoh.

Two tiny mummies found in the tomb with him, for example, suggest that Tutankhamun might have had two stillborn daughters. When scientists examined the mummy of Tutankhamun himself, they worked out that he must have had some medical problems (he had special shoes and 130 walking sticks!), but we still don't know why he died so young.

The pictures on a decorated fan found in the tomb show that rich Egyptians like Tutankhamun enjoyed hunting ostriches. They also loved showing off items made from precious materials, and one of Carter's most extraordinary finds is a dagger made with metal from a meteorite that is billions of years old.

Like us, Egyptians liked to relax sometimes as well. Tutankhamun was buried with board games made of carved ivory and two musical instruments called sistrums. He had boomerangs too, which may have been used

to bring down birds while he was sailing down the River Nile.

The boomerangs and the sistrums are not as glittery and exciting as the boy-pharaoh's golden mask and golden bed, but they are just as valuable to the historians who are trying to understand how life was lived on the banks of the Nile more than 3,000 years ago. We may not know how Tutankhamun died, but his tomb and its treasures will continue to reveal more and more secrets of Egyptian life in the days of its most famous pharaoh.

Bringing incredible
TRUE STORIES
to life ...

AN INCREDIBLE TRUE STORY

TRAGEDY AT
SEA
The Sinking of the Titanic

Illustrated by
STEFANO
TAMBELLINI

ISBN: 978-1-78112-966-1

AN INCREDIBLE TRUE STORY

DAVID
LONG

SURVIVAL IN
SPACE
The Apollo 13 Mission

Illustrated by
STEFANO
TAMBELLINI

ISBN: 978-1-78112-938-8

www.davidlong.info

Our books are tested
for children and young people by
children and young people.

Thanks to everyone who consulted on
a manuscript for their time and effort in
helping us to make our books better
for our readers.